This book is dedicated to my Mom, Patricia Humphrey,
who has never given up on me.

I would like to thank my family and friends
who have encouraged me for the past two years to
finish this book.

Special thanks to my niece, Rebecca Schaefer,
on doing the photography
for the back cover and last page of the book.

This book is based on a real story about how Abbey lived
her first couple years before I adopted her. She was probably never
physically abused, but severely neglected. I hope that all readers will
get insight on how a pet feels when there is no love in their life.
It's a very sad situation.
Your pet needs more than food and water.
They need you to love them and protect them.

I'm not perceptive enough to understand what animals
are saying, so some of the dialogue in this book is imagined.
I can say that Abbey had very real communication
with every other animal in this story though.

The people in this townhouse community
pulled together as a group to help Abbey
in her times of need.
It was a beautiful thing to see people of all different
situations come together to help one little cat.

Abbey is still with me today and I'm happy to report
that she is a very spoiled and contented cat.

ABBEY THE TOWNHOUSE CAT

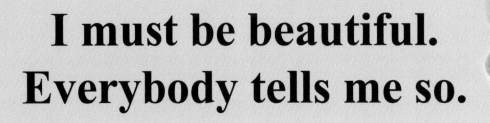

I must be beautiful.
Everybody tells me so.

I'm different than the other cats.
They have only one place to go
to be safe.

Everyone invites me in.
They all want to pet me and feed me,
and they try to
make me love them.

I should be a happy cat
with all of this attention.

But this is where I live!

Why can't I come in?
Just for a few minutes
to get something to eat.

I can see that you are home.
The lights are on.

Oh please...
I want to come in now.

That's alright.

I'd rather be out here
anyway.

I can find someone to
play with.

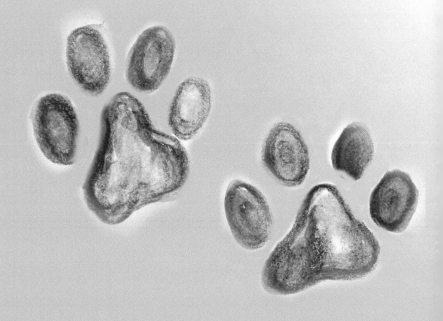

Oh...Hi Abbey.

Sorry. I can't play chase
with you now.

It's getting dark and wet and
scary out here.

Don't you have somewhere to
go home to?

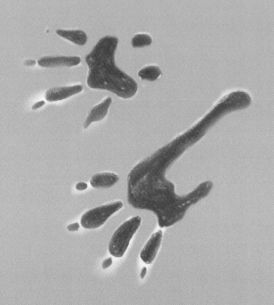

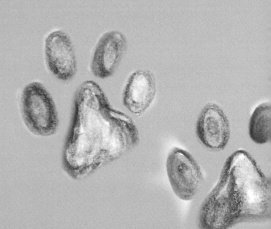

See you later
Mr. Squirrel.

Where am I going to go
now? It's not much fun
out here when there's
no one to chase around.

I'll go around to the place
where the people park.
Someone will take
me in and feed me.

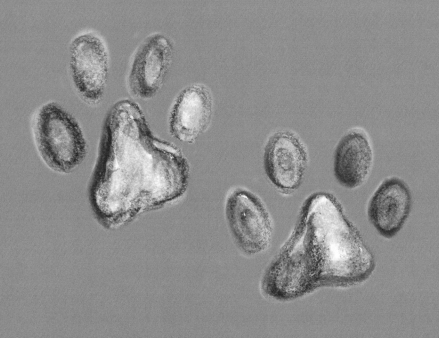

Oh Abbey!

Are you out here alone
and hungry?
You can come home with me.

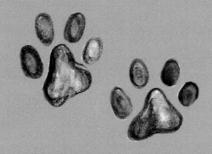

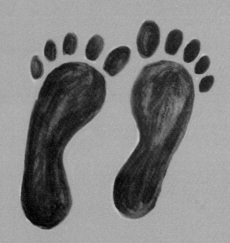

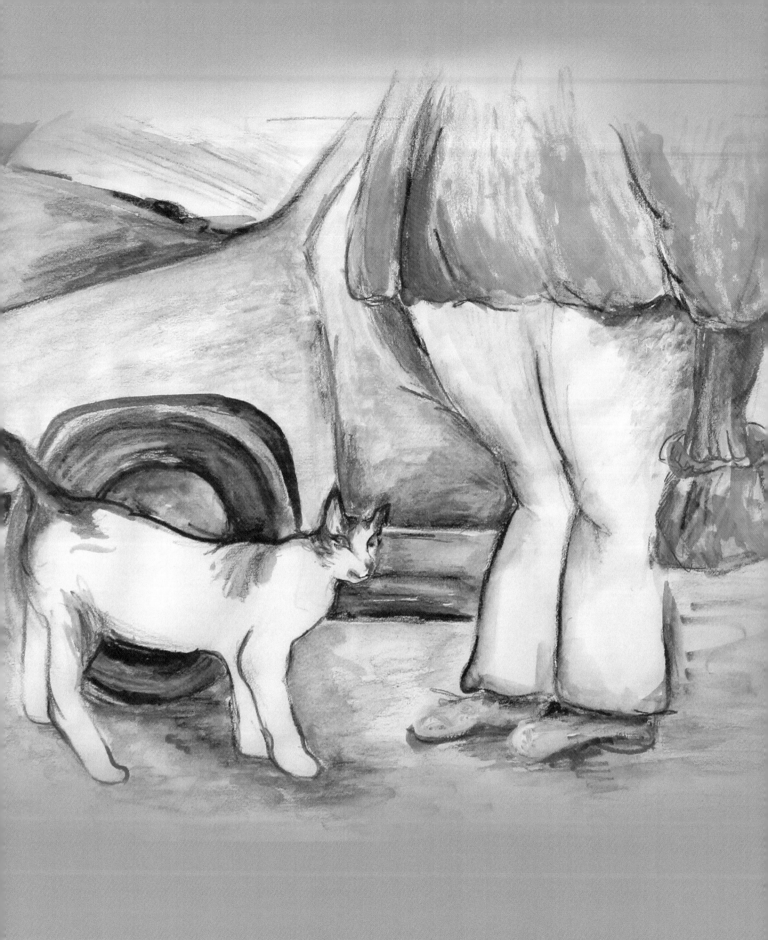

We're sharing our dinner
with Abbey again.

I found her outside
alone and hungry.

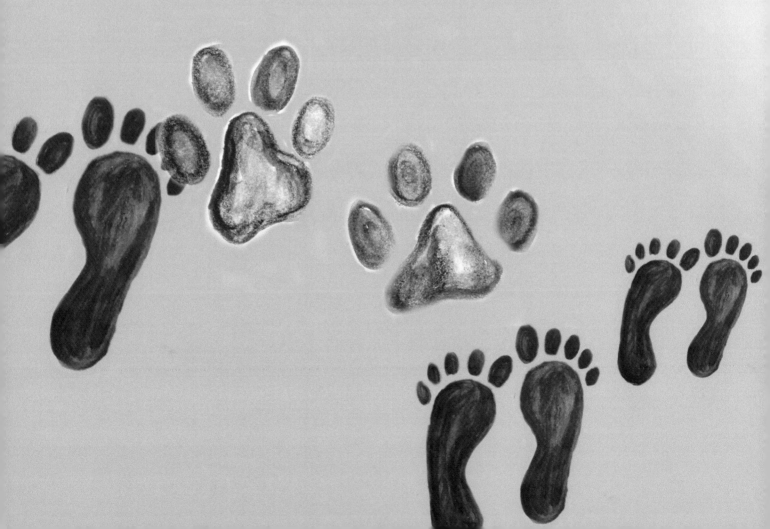

Mr. Blue Jay, where do you sleep at night?

Sometimes I can't find somewhere to go, and my people keep leaving me out at night.

Can I come up there with you?

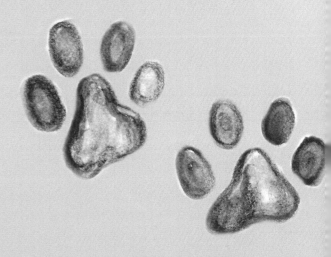

I sleep in the trees.
You can't do that, Abbey.
You might fall out, and cats
DON'T always land on their feet.

I wish you could find a new
family to love you and
take care of you.

Look Mom!

It's Abbey. She looks
lonely. It must be our turn
to take care of her.

Can I pretty, pretty please
bring her in?

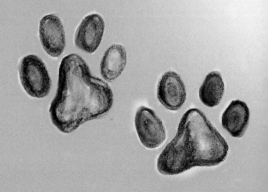

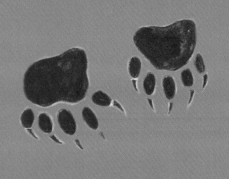
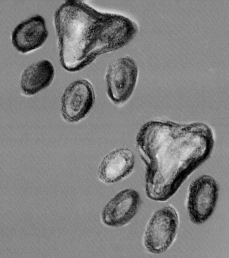

Mr. Skunk

Why aren't you scared
to be out here alone
all night?

I'm a skunk. People don't want
me in their house.
You're a cat.
You shouldn't be outside alone.
And it's getting colder.
We might have snow soon.

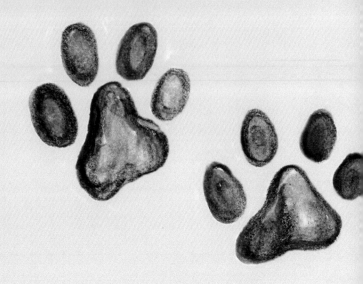

Oh N0!

Please don't make me
go out. It's cold out and
it's starting to snow.

I don't like to get wet.

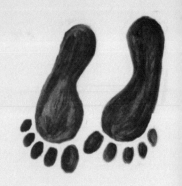

Lady, why do you hurt
Abbey?

How would you like it if
I took off your clothes
and left you out in the
snow all night?

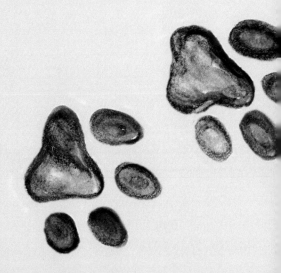

Abbey, I'm so sorry that
you cannot stay with me.

It's only because I have to
travel so much and you
would be left alone.

I'm going to talk to the
other neighbors and try
to find someone
to help you.

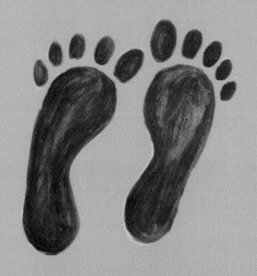
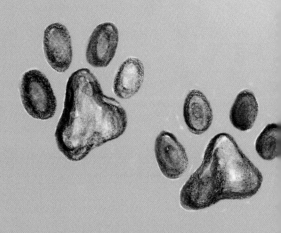

Poor Abbey!

Can any of us adopt her?

I already have three cats at my house.

I'm out of town for work
all the time.
She needs someone who can
love her all the time.

I've got my parents
staying with me and my
husband and three kids.
I just don't have the room.

What am I going to do?

Everybody loves me.
But nobody loves me enough to
let me live with them.

I might as well just run away.

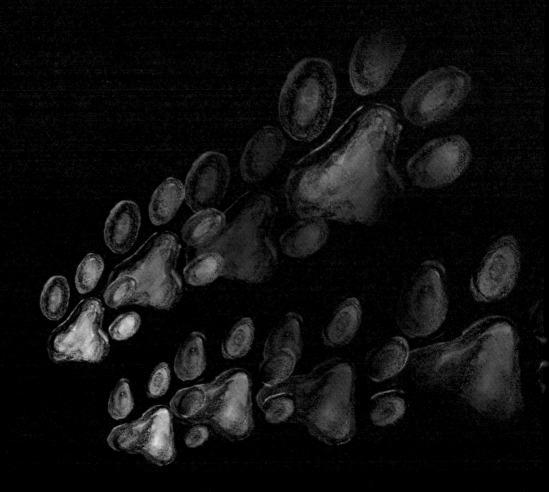

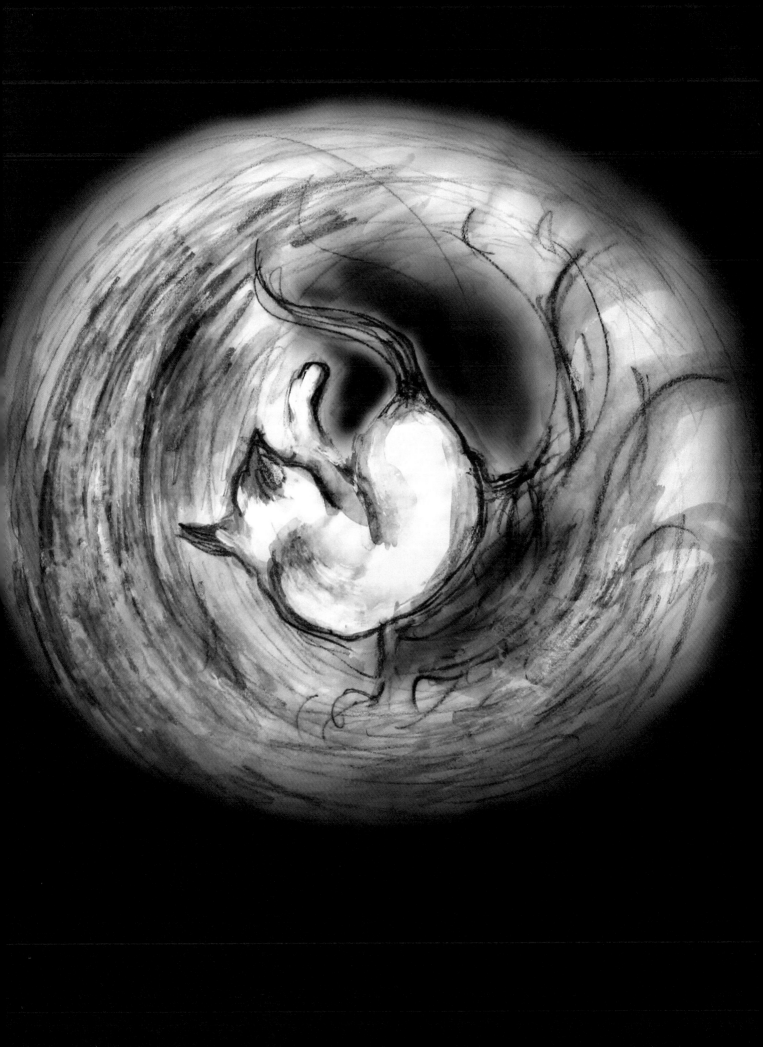

This MIGHT not be a good idea.

I've never crossed the street before.

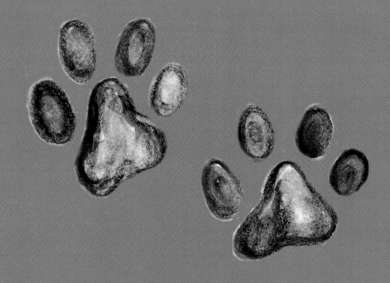

I can run
faster than you.

I can outrun
ANYONE!

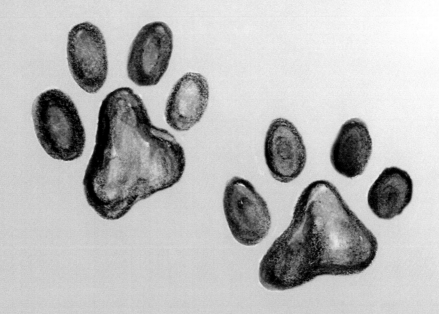

I don't know what
THAT was, but
I'm okay now.

I'm very well hidden.

But where am I?

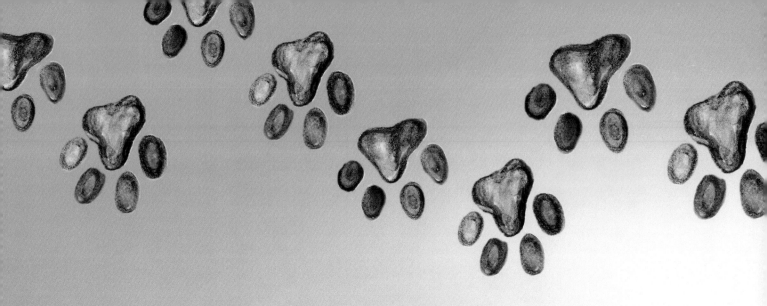

Who are you, and
how did you end up here?

My name is Abbey.
I live in all the townhouses.
But I think I lost the townhouses.

And they don't want me anymore.
Can I stay with you?

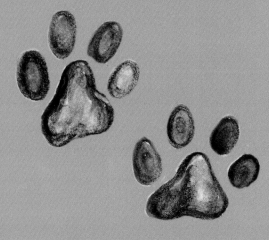

I live in all
the townhouses.

But I wish I could have
just one home to call my own.

I did a long time ago.
Let me tell you....

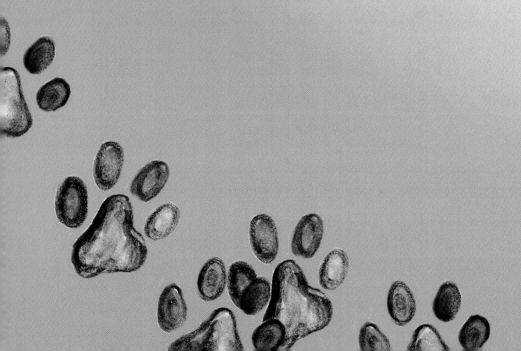

It was just me and my Daddy.

He loved me and
I felt safe and
happy.

Then SHE came to stay
with us.

She didn't pet me or
love me.

And she made me go outside
every time my Daddy was gone.

I must have been a
very bad kitty to have been
punished so much.

I don't know what I did wrong.
She just didn't want me
to be with her.

Hi. Welcome to the townhouses.
Say, do you have a cat,
or would you like to?

Hmmm....

Because there is a little (mostly)
white cat that we all look after.
She's been missing for a few days now,
and we're very worried about her.

I'll watch out for her.
I'm alone and would love to
have her stay with me.

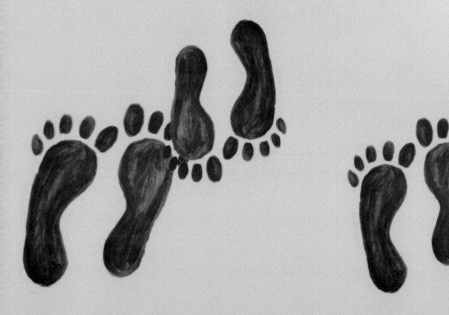

Sometimes I like to be outside.

But I want to come in when
it's cold and rainy.

I get scared and
sad to be
left all alone.

I was left alone so much!

Abbey, I have good news!

There's a new human living at the townhouses, and she WANTS YOU!

All of your other human friends are worried about you, and they told her about you.

Hurry, we have to get you home now.

Come on Abbey.

We'll get you home safely.

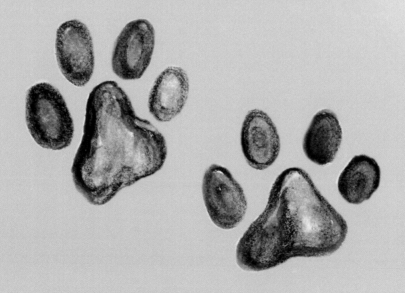

Abbey

crossing the

Road

with a little help
from her friends.

Could it be?

Is that my new Momma
in the doorway?

Oh, I'm just going to
LEAP through
that door, and
go to her now.

Here I come Momma!

I'm in LOVE!

I am

HOME

About the Author

Kathy Musick was born in Detroit, Michigan.
Other than a few years in the US Army and another few
in NYC, she has lived in Southeast Michigan.

Kathy studied painting, sculture and printmaking at
the University of Michigan, School of Art in Ann Arbor.
She continues to draw and paint
when Abbey doesn't need attention!

You can contact Kathy and Abbey at
abbeythetownhousecat@yahoo.com

CPSIA information can be obtained at www.ICGtesting.com
Printed in the USA
LVIW01n1032191216
517925LV00008B/108